To Mom and Dad and Luke, and

also all my lovely friends. — J. W.

A Tiger Without Stripes

JAIMIE WHITBREAD

There was a tiger

who had sharp claws,

and golden eyes,

and velvet fur.

But when other tigers looked at her,

the only thing that they could see

was that she had no stripes.

"It doesn't matter," said her mother.

"It doesn't matter," said her brothers.

But it mattered.

To a tiger with no stripes, it mattered,

because she was the one
who had none.

Maybe they are out there somewhere, the tiger thought.

Maybe I have not looked hard enough.

Maybe I must earn them.

And so she went to try.

The sun beat down and blazed hot.

"But I can face the sun, no matter how blazing."

And the sun painted stripes across the tiger's back.

"I've found them!" said the tiger.

But when the sun faded,
the stripes faded, too.

The forest grew thick, and dark, and close.

"But I can brave the forest, no matter how thick."

And the forest scratched stripes into her skin.

"I've found them!" said the tiger.

But when the scrapes healed,

the stripes healed, too.

Wind and rain thrashed the rocks.

"But I can stand the wind, I can stand the rain."

And the rain ran down her coat in stripes.

"I've found them!" said the tiger.

But when the rain dried, the stripes dried, too.

Finally the tiger went as high, high as she could go,

to where she knew she would be heard,

and she shouted to the sky:

"Why?"

"Every other tiger

is given stripes.

Just given stripes.

They don't have to face the sun.

They don't have to brave the forest.

They don't have to stand the rain.

I have done all three – but where are my stripes?

Haven't I earned them yet?"

To her surprise, a voice replied,

"I have made the tigers, all the tigers, every one,

 and only I can tell you:

A tiger does not earn its stripes.

They are a gift."

"Then what did you give me?" asked the tiger.

"What is my gift?"

But there was no reply.

The tiger could not say a word.

She hung her head.

She went away to a lonely place.

"But what did you give me?

What did you give me?"

She thought about it all night long.

About the stripes that she would never have.

About the sun,

and the woods,

and the rain.

The next day the tiger went back.

She went to the high, high place and said,

"Thank you."

"Why do you thank me?" asked the voice.

"Because of what you gave me," the tiger said.

"And what did I give you?"

"You made all the tigers, every tiger,

and when you made me, you made me without stripes.

And because I had no stripes,

I went to look for them."

"I faced the sun.

I braved the forest.

I felt the wind."

"I heard your voice."

"So when the other tigers say,

You have sharp claws,

and golden eyes,

and velvet fur –

what a shame you

have no stripes,

I will tell them No —"

"What a gift!"

Library of Congress Control Number: 2019947267
ISBN 9781943147717

Text copyright © 2020 by Jaimie Whitbread
Illustrations copyright © 2020 Jaimie Whitbread

Published by The Innovation Press
1001 4th Avenue, Suite 3200, Seattle, WA 98154
www.theinnovationpress.com

Printed and bound by Worzalla
Production date October 2019

Cover lettering by Nicole LaRue
Cover art by Jaimie Whitbread
Book layout by Tim Martyn